The
SUPREME
COURT

The SUPREME COURT

by Barbara Aria

★ ★ ★

Franklin Watts
New York / Chicago / London / Toronto / Sydney
A First Book

Cover photograph copyright © Donna Rowe-Hurt/Washington Stock Photo, Inc.

Photographs copyright ©: Collection of the Supreme Court of the United States: pp. 6, 11 (both Franz Jantzen), 25, 28 (John B. Martin), 41 (*National Geographic*), 45 (Charles Sidney Hopkinson); UPI/Bettmann: pp. 12, 34 top, 43, 49, 50, 51; The Bettmann Archive: pp. 13, 15, 21, 29, 48, 53; Virginia Museum of Fine Arts, Richmond Va.: p. 16; National Archives: p. 17; Wide World Photos: pp. 19, 34 bottom, 35, 38 bottom, 46, 55; North Wind Picture Archives, Alfred, Me.: pp. 26, 40; New York Public Library, Picture Collection: pp. 30, 31; Jay Mallin: p. 38 top; Supreme Court Historical Society: p. 54; Reuters/Bettmann: p. 56.

Library of Congress Cataloging-in-Publication Data

Aria, Barbara.
    The Supreme Court / Barbara Aria.
    p. cm. — (A First book)
    Includes bibliographical references and index.
      ISBN 0-531-20180-5
        1. United States. Supreme Court—Juvenile literature.
    2. Judicial power—United States—Juvenile literature.
    I. Title. II. Series.
    KF8742.Z9A75 1994
    347.73'26—dc20   94-979
    [347.30735]   CIP   AC

Contents

Chapter 1

What Is the Supreme Court?

If you watch the evening news on television, or read the newspaper, you might come across a headline story that begins, "The Supreme Court ruled today . . ." And you might find yourself wondering, "What is the Supreme Court? Why is everyone so interested in what happens there?"

If you ask these questions out loud, you'll probably be told that the Supreme Court is where final judgments are made about the laws of the United States and about people's rights under the law.

The Supreme Court is a part of the United States government. Its home is in Washington, D.C., in a building so grand that it has been nicknamed "the Marble Palace." Here the nine judges, or justices, of the Supreme Court meet to decide many of the questions facing the people of this country. During its history, the Supreme Court has made decisions on questions of slavery, free speech, women's rights, children's rights, racial discrimination, and many others. These decisions have become a part of the law under which we live, affecting the day-to-day lives of millions of Americans.

The United States Supreme Court is the highest court of law in the land. Even the president has to obey its rulings. Like an ordinary law court, the Supreme Court settles arguments between people or between an individual and the government. And, like any other law court, it can only settle an argument that is presented in the form of a criminal or civil case. In a criminal case, someone is accused of breaking the law. In a civil case, two people or groups of people go to court to settle a dispute; perhaps they both claim ownership of a certain piece of land, or perhaps an employee claims that he or she has been unfairly treated by an employer.

. . .the Supreme Court ruled that all prayer was illegal in public schools.

Imagine if one of your teachers lost her job because she was pregnant. That used to happen frequently. Then, in 1970, a junior high school teacher who had been fired from her job because she was pregnant brought a civil case against her employer, the school board. The teacher said that this was a case of discrimination, because she was perfectly able to teach while she was pregnant. Her employer argued that teaching was exhausting and that it was dangerous for the woman's health and for that of her unborn child.

Who do you think was right, the teacher or her employer? That was the question the Supreme Court justices had to decide.

Only certain kinds of cases can be heard by the Supreme Court. The case of the pregnant teacher was one that concerned the Court because it involved a question of constitutional rights. The Supreme Court decided that this teacher had the right to keep working even though she was pregnant, because the Fourteenth Amendment to the Constitution guarantees all citizens the liberty to make choices about their personal life.

The Court's decision meant that pregnant employees throughout the United States would have the legal right to keep working for as long as they were able to do their job. When the Supreme Court makes a decision, or ruling, that ruling applies to everyone, not just to the people involved in the case.

Why is the Supreme Court so powerful? Because it has the final say—after the lower courts, Congress, and even the president—about what is legal. For instance, in 1958 the Court ruled on whether or not it is legal for children to have prayer time in public schools. A father took this case to the Supreme Court after he discovered that his child's teacher was leading the class in prayer every morning. He believed that his child had the right to grow up making his own choices about God and religion.

The school board, the state, and the lower courts all felt that it was okay for the teacher to lead her class in prayer, because no child was forced to pray. But the Supreme Court ruled that all prayer was illegal in public schools.

The Court's decision in this case had nothing to do with whether or not the justices personally believed that it was a good or a bad thing for children to say prayers in school. In fact, Supreme Court justices pray together before they begin work each morning. But prayer in public schools, they said, goes against the Constitution, which states that all Americans, however young, should be free to practice whatever religion they choose, without the government interfering.

The Supreme Court's special job is to make sure that the Constitution of the United States is upheld by the branches of the government. If the Court finds that a state law or an act of Congress goes against the Constitution, then that law or act can no longer stand. Even a presidential act can be found unlawful by the Supreme Court.

The Supreme Court is there for every citizen, rich or poor, young or old. That is what is meant by the words inscribed over the entrance to the Marble Palace: "Equal

Above the entrance to the Supreme Court are the words "Equal Justice Under Law."

Justice Under Law." Most of the cases decided by the Supreme Court involve ordinary people, including children. Because of Supreme Court rulings, children are no longer segregated into separate schools according to race, and students in public schools no longer pray. They are not forced to salute the flag, and they can no longer be suspended from school just for wearing antiwar slogans or other political messages.

(opposite page) The ending of the segregation of black and white school-children is but one of the important decisions handed down by the Supreme Court. (above) For much of U.S. history children were required to salute the flag at the beginning of each school day. (left) Before desegregation black children studied in separate schools such as this one in rural Georgia in 1941.

You or your parents might not agree with some Supreme Court decisions. Millions of Americans, the president, and many congressmen have disagreed with the Court's ruling on school prayer. They hope that someday the Court will change this ruling. Often the Court does change, or reverse, an earlier ruling.

The Court does not have the power to make people obey its rulings. It has to rely on the government and citizens to carry them out. Nevertheless, most people feel that if we believe in living by the Constitution, then as President John F. Kennedy once said, "It's important that we support the Supreme Court decisions, even when we may not agree with them."

Chapter 2 ★ ★ ★

The Constitution and the Supreme Court

Charles Evans Hughes, a former Supreme Court chief justice, once said that the Constitution is whatever the Supreme Court says it is. He meant that the Supreme Court has the power to decide, for all Americans, what the words of the Constitution really mean.

Justice Hughes likened the Supreme Court to the umpire in a baseball game. The umpire decides whether to call a player safe or out. Even if most of the people watching the ball game disagree with the call, the umpire's decision is final and goes on record. One of the Court's jobs is to referee disagreements between states, and between state governments and the federal government.

The Supreme Court is the most important umpire in the country, because rather than talking about a

Chief Justice Charles Evans Hughes

strike or ball, it is talking about the Constitution, which is the nation's rule book for how the government works. The United States Constitution has been called the "supreme law of the land." Every law made in this country must agree with it.

Every nation has its own idea of what freedoms and rights its citizens should have and how these rights and powers can be protected. In the United States these rules are set out in the Constitution. Our Constitution was made law two hundred years ago, and it is still law today.

Washington Addressing the Constitutional Convention, *an oil painting by Junius Brutus Stearns.*

The people who wrote, or framed, the Constitution wanted to be sure that no one person or group of people would ever gain too much power. So they set out three separate branches of government, each of which would keep a check on the other's power. The Congress, or legislative branch, makes laws. The executive branch, led by the president, carries out laws. The judicial branch, made up of the courts of law and headed by the Supreme Court, makes sure that the Congress and the president keep within the powers given to them by the Constitution.

The framers didn't want the Constitution to become outdated, so they decided that Congress could occasionally add to, or amend, it as times changed. Almost as soon as the Constitution was approved by the states, the Congress approved ten amendments.

The original hand-written copy of the U.S. Constitution, now on display at the National Archives in Washington, D.C.

These first ten amendments are known as the Bill of Rights. They were designed to guarantee all citizens certain individual rights, or freedoms, such as the right to free speech.

The Founding Fathers knew that sometimes a powerful group of people might try to take away the rights of another group. They gave the Supreme Court the job of making sure that the constitutional rights of citizens were protected. Over time, this job gave the Court a very special role in shaping the private lives of Americans.

However, the Constitution could not settle all of the questions about what is lawful and what is not. For a start, quite often the same words mean different things to different people. Imagine if someone said, "You must be polite to your teachers." You and your mother might disagree about what *polite* really means, and a time traveler from two hundred years ago would have a third, different idea of the word's meaning.

The Constitution uses many words and phrases that have uncertain meanings. For instance, the Eighth Amendment states that there should be no "cruel and unusual punishment" of prisoners. But what kind of punishment is "cruel and unusual"? When these words were written, it wasn't unusual for a criminal to be whipped, branded with a red-hot iron, or chained by the ankle to a heavy metal ball. Some convicts even had their ears cut off. Today these punishments

The burning of the U.S. flag is protected under the Constitution as an expression of free speech.

seem both cruel and unusual. In recent years Supreme Court justices have been asked to decide whether the death sentence for criminals counts as cruel and unusual punishment.

The Supreme Court's understanding of the Constitution is called an interpretation. The Court has had to decide many cases involving interpretations of the First Amendment, which guarantees citizens the right to freedom of speech. What does "freedom of speech" mean? How free can speech be? What kind of speech is protected by law?

In 1968 a man publicly burned an American flag in New York after he heard that a civil rights leader had been shot. He was very angry that his country could have let the shooting happen. New York State law said that it was illegal to mutilate the flag, so the man was charged with a crime. But the Supreme Court said that when the man burned the flag, he was expressing his feelings about his country, just as if he were using speech. Therefore, according to the Court, symbolic acts such as burning the flag are protected under the First Amendment and cannot be called illegal.

The Supreme Court's interpretations are very important for all Americans. When the Court ruled in favor of the child whose father didn't want him saying prayers in school, newspapers all over the country carried headlines like "School Prayer Unconstitutional."

Teachers in many schools had been praying with their classes, but now prayer had been ruled to be illegal in all public schools. If another parent sued a school board for the same reason, a lower court would have to follow the Supreme Court's ruling. This is what is known as precedent (a word that comes from "to precede," or "to go before"). Once a decision has been made by the Court, that decision is carried over to every similar case, until the Supreme Court makes a new ruling on the same question. In this way, people know what to expect from the law.

The Supreme Court has the huge responsibility of trying to make wise decisions that follow the spirit of the Constitution. But the justices don't always agree on how the Constitution should be interpreted. Some believe that it's important to try to figure out what the framers meant when they wrote the Constitution. Other justices believe the Court should be guided by the Constitution's actual words. Some justices believe that they can make a difference in people's lives by looking for ways to rule certain laws unconstitutional. Those who disagree say that lawmaking is the job of the elected Congress and that the Court should interfere only when absolutely necessary.

Though they may have different guiding ideas or philosophies, Supreme Court justices are expected to make decisions without being influenced by their personal beliefs or interests. But the justices are still regular people after they have put on their judges' hats and long black robes. They have particular points of view and allegiances that can influence their thinking.

One of the Court's worst decisions was made in 1857 in a now famous case known as *Scott* v. *Sanford* (the v. stands for "versus," or "against"). Dred Scott, who brought the case to the Supreme Court, was a slave. He had lived for a while with his master in the territory of Wisconsin, where slavery had been barred by Congress. After returning to Missouri, Dred Scott sued for his freedom.

Dred Scott

He reasoned that he had become free when he entered Wisconsin, a territory where slavery was not allowed.

As people waited for the Court's decision, the United States was trying to avoid a civil war between states that were for slavery and those that were against it. Congress had created free territories like Wisconsin and let some states keep slaves, in the hope that such a compromise would bring peace.

After the Supreme Court announced its decision, it seemed as if war could not be avoided. The Court said that the Constitution did not give any rights to African Americans, whether or not they were slaves. A slave or freed slave was not a citizen. The Court also said that according to the Constitution, Congress could not declare territories like Wisconsin free from slavery, because that would take away a slave owner's right to his "property." Why did the Court make this decision? One reason was that many of the justices on the Court came from slave states and might themselves have been slave owners.

. . . a slave or a freed slave was not a citizen.

However, this was not the end of the Court's Dred Scott decision. The Congress can "overrule" a Supreme Court decision by amending the Constitution. This has happened only four times in the history of the Court. In 1868, Congress passed the Fourteenth Amendment, overturning the Supreme Court's *Scott* v. *Sanford*. This amendment said that all former slaves were citizens, and that all citizens have an equal right to be protected by the law.

Chapter 3

How the Supreme Court Grew and Changed

When the framers of the Constitution wrote about the three branches of government, they wrote very little about the judicial branch. They had already spent weeks arguing about the powers of the executive and legislative branches, and they knew there would be more arguments about the judicial branch. They were impatient to have their new Constitution approved by the states.

So for the time being, the framers simply wrote, "The judicial power of the United States shall be vested in one Supreme Court, and in such inferior courts as the Congress shall from time to time ordain and establish." Then they explained that the Supreme Court would handle cases involving the Constitution and laws made by Congress. The framers left most of the rest up to Congress.

On a cold day in February 1790, the Supreme Court justices gathered for the first time in their temporary home in New York City. It was a solemn occasion. The newspapers reported on the gathering and told people about their new branch of government.

But many questions about the role of the Supreme Court

The first and temporary home of the U.S. Supreme Court in New York City

were left unanswered. Would the Supreme Court have power over the president? How much power would the Court have over state courts and over acts of Congress? Alexander Hamilton argued that the job of *judicial review*— deciding whether a state or federal law is constitutional—belonged to the Supreme Court. But Thomas Jefferson and James Madison said that this job belonged to the individual states.

In the beginning, few people thought that the United States Supreme Court would ever be very powerful. In fact, there were supposed to be six justices sitting at that first session of the Supreme Court, but only four showed up. One justice said he didn't want the job because it wasn't important enough.

Alexander Hamilton (top), James Madison (above left), and Thomas Jefferson (left)

Another justice never once attended the Court. After being absent for three terms, he resigned.

Some of the early sessions of the Court were held in cramped temporary quarters. For a while the justices had to meet in a tavern! During the first twelve years of the Supreme Court, the justices heard only sixty cases—an average of five a year (nowadays they hear almost two hundred a year). They were very careful not to make any decisions that would step on the toes of Congress, the president, or the states. They didn't know if people would accept such interference from the Court. Then, in 1803, the Court finally declared an act of Congress unconstitutional—a procedure known as judicial review—in a case called *Marbury* v. *Madison.*

William Marbury had been promised an important government position by outgoing president John Adams. The new president, Thomas Jefferson, refused to honor that promise. Marbury decided to take his case directly to the Supreme Court. He believed he was entitled to do this by the Judiciary Act, which Congress had recently passed into law.

Chief Justice John Marshall said although Marbury should be given his position, the Court had no power to rule on this matter. According to the Constitution, he said, a case like this had to be heard by a lower court first, even though the

Judiciary Act disagreed. Of course, this meant that the Judiciary Act violated the Constitution and could not stand as written. Many people argued that the Supreme Court was not entitled to tell Congress its law was unconstitutional, but eventually the Court's power of judicial review was accepted.

Chief Justice John Marshall

By acting as an umpire in the important arguments of its times, the Court grew even more powerful. At first, the biggest question was: who has the greater power, the individual states or the federal government? Can a state have laws that don't agree with the Constitution? The Supreme Court said that state laws have to agree with the Constitution because the Constitution was created not by individual states but by "the people of the United States."

After the Civil War, the Fourteenth Amendment guaranteed the rights of freed slaves in all the states. But many states still tried to keep African Americans powerless by introducing laws saying that schools and other public facilities had to be racially segregated. A former slave named Homer Plessy was arrested for sitting in an all-white railroad car in Louisiana. He appealed to the Supreme Court, claiming that he had been denied his constitutional right to equality. The Court said that it was possible for a facility to be "separate but equal." Because of this ruling, segregation continued for many years.

Railroad cars, just like most public facilities, were segregated for many years under the "separate but equal" ruling of the Supreme Court.

Meanwhile, the nation was growing quickly. America was becoming a country of factories rather than farms. Some people thought that government should protect workers who were toiling long hours in dark, hot, airless factories. States passed laws to make employers provide better working conditions. But the factory owners appealed to the Supreme Court, claiming that the government had no constitutional right to interfere in their

affairs. The Court agreed. Businesses, it said, have a constitutional right to make whatever kind of arrangement they like with their employees. For much of its history, the Court tried hard to protect the rights of businesses and paid little attention to the rights of individuals.

Some of the people who suffered because of the Court's decisions were children. Factory owners liked to employ children because they weren't paid as much as adults. Boys and girls as young as ten were spending long hours at jobs that

(left) Young children worked in deplorable conditions such as in this coal mine and on farms picking crops (below) until the Supreme Court finally upheld a law enacted by Congress regulating labor practices.

were dangerous and unhealthy. Congress passed laws to regulate child labor, but businessmen objected and soon the Supreme Court overturned the laws.

During the Great Depression, millions of Americans were unemployed, and families were going hungry. In 1936, Franklin D. Roosevelt was elected to his second term as president. A huge majority of the people had voted for his "New Deal" for Americans. They wanted government to step in and help make America a fair country where workers and their families would be protected. By now everyone knew that the Supreme Court had the power to support or reject Roosevelt's New Deal policies.

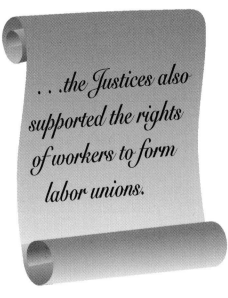

. . .the Justices also supported the rights of workers to form labor unions.

Finally the Court paid attention to the terrible state of the nation and to the people who were suffering. It found new ways of interpreting the Constitution. The Court upheld a new law that said women and children had to be paid a minimum wage. The justices also voted to uphold the rights of workers to form labor unions.

Soon the Supreme Court began using its power to protect the rights of individuals in their private lives. It changed, or reversed, some of its earlier rulings. The Supreme Court has reversed itself about a hundred times since it first sat in session. These reversals show how the Court has reinterpreted the Constitution to stay in tune with the times.

In 1954 the Supreme Court took a new look at the question of segregation. Ever since the 1896 ruling that approved of "separate but equal" facilities for blacks, African Americans had been segregated in every area of life. When Linda Brown, elementary school student, was denied the right to attend an all-white school in her neighborhood, her father decided to take the case to court. He didn't see why she had to cross a railroad yard, catch a bus, and travel for forty-five minutes to an all-black school.

By now it was obvious to most people that many schools for African American children were not as good as white schools, because they were poorer. After considering the case of *Brown* v. *Board of Education*, the Court decided that separate was not equal. Their decision soon made all racial segregation illegal.

The Court decision that required integration of schools was Brown v. Board of Education. *At left, Linda Brown returns as an adult to the elementary school she sued to attend.*

The issue of busing as a result of the Court's decision to end segregation of public schools immediately became volatile. Police were often required to escort black children into the formerly all-white schools.

Chapter 4

How the Supreme Court Works Today

*I*n 1968 fourteen-year-old Mary Beth Tinker found herself in the Supreme Court, where her lawyer was defending her case against her local school district.

How did Mary Beth end up in the Court? What had to happen before her case could be heard by the justices? And how did the Court make its decision?

Very few cases can be taken directly to the Supreme Court. The Court has original jurisdiction, or first hearing, only in cases involving conflicts between states. In most cases, the Supreme Court acts as an appeals court. If a person is unhappy with the decision of a lower court, he or she can appeal, or ask for a new decision from a higher court.

It can take quite a while between the time when a person first brings a case to a lower court and the time when the Supreme Court announces its final decision in the case. Two and a half years passed between Mary Beth's first appearance in a federal district court and the Supreme Court's final decision in her case in February 1969.

It all started in December 1965, when Mary Beth Tinker decided to protest the war in Vietnam by wearing a black armband to her school in Des Moines, Iowa. When Mary Beth walked into her algebra class with her armband on, she was immediately sent to the principal's office and suspended from school. Within a few days several more students were suspended from Des Moines schools for wearing armbands.

The students, together with some of their parents, decided to fight the school authorities' rule against armbands. They called the American Civil Liberties Union. The ACLU is an organization that gives free legal help to people who want to defend their constitutional rights.

The ACLU took the children's case to court in Des Moines, suing the school board in federal district court (a local court where criminal and civil cases involving federal laws are first heard). The district judge decided that the school board's ban on armbands was reasonable. He said that wearing armbands in school could disrupt order in the classroom.

The ACLU decided to help the students appeal the decision in a higher court. The appeal was heard in federal appeals court the next year, in 1967. (A federal appeals court reconsiders decisions handed down by a district court.)

Half of the appeals court judges voted in favor of Mary Beth, and the other half voted in favor of the school board. So the appeals court asked the Supreme Court to decide. If the court had decided in favor of the school board, Mary

Today's Supreme Court chambers (above) and the chambers used by the Court during the nineteenth century inside the U.S. Capitol (left)

Beth could have appealed for a final decision in the Supreme Court.

About five thousand cases find their way to the Supreme Court every year, but the justices have time to hear only about two hundred of these cases. The justices look through all the cases and decide which are the most important. At least four justices must agree to hear a case. Otherwise it is rejected.

Mary Beth Tinker's case went on the list of cases the justices wanted to hear. At least three months went by before the hearing. During that time the lawyers on the case had to supply the Court with briefs. A brief includes a record of the lower court's testimony and a statement about why the lawyer thinks the court's ruling was wrong or right.

. . . the students had the right to exercise free speech through the use of symbols.

Finally, in November 1968, the justices heard arguments in the case. The Supreme Court hears arguments in the courtroom of the Marble Palace. The justices listen to the lawyers on both sides of the case and also to experts who the lawyers think can help support their arguments. The individuals involved in the case do not speak, but they can attend the courtroom hearings.

First, the ACLU lawyer spoke for Mary Beth. He argued that schools should be tolerant of students who want to express their opinions through symbols that don't disrupt the class. He also pointed out that students had been allowed to wear buttons supporting presidential candidates. If they could wear political buttons, then why couldn't they wear armbands? Then, the lawyer for the school board took his turn, arguing that schools can't wait for disorder to break out before they do something. They have to stop it before it happens.

The taking of photographs within the Supreme Court chambers is not allowed while the court is in session. This is an artist's engraving of a case being tried before the justices earlier this century.

Chief Justice Earl Warren

After hearing arguments in the case, the justices had a conference to discuss it. Supreme Court conferences are secret. Nobody is allowed to enter the room while the justices are talking.

Usually the chief justice begins the discussion. Chief Justice Earl Warren argued that because the school authorities had allowed students to wear political buttons, they could not stop other students from wearing armbands. But he said that the First Amendment was more important in this case. The students had the right to exercise free speech through symbols, just like the man who burned the flag. Other justices disagreed and presented their reasons. Then a vote was taken on whether the Court should uphold or overturn the lower court's ruling against Mary Beth. The majority voted to overturn it.

After the justices have voted, the most senior member of the majority chooses a justice to write a majority opinion, and a dissenting, or disagreeing, judge writes the minority opinion. If a justice agrees with the decision but not with the reasons that led to it, he or she can write a concurring opinion.

The justices' words are carefully chosen, and writing an opinion can take weeks or even months. Law clerks help by gathering the necessary information. Once written, these opinions are printed and given to all the justices to read. The justices hope their opinions will persuade other justices to change sides. Often a justice who disagreed at first will suggest how an opinion could be rewritten to meet with his or her approval.

When all the justices have read the opinions and discussed them, they vote again to see if anyone has changed sides. This last vote is final. The justices hearing Mary Beth Tinker's case voted 7–2 to overrule the lower court's decision. More than three years had passed since Mary Beth was suspended from school. But she knew she had won for all students a guarantee that they would no longer have to "shed their constitutional rights at the schoolhouse gate," as Justice Abe Fortas wrote in his opinion for the majority.

Justice Abe Fortas was appointed to the Supreme Court by President Lyndon B. Johnson.

Chapter 5

The Supreme Court Justices

One of the few things that the Constitution says about the Supreme Court is that its members, unlike members of the legislative and executive branches, are not elected. They are chosen by the president, with the "advice and consent" of the Senate, and they can sit on the Court for life as long as they show "good behavior." Most justices serve for as long as they can physically and mentally do their job. Justice Oliver Wendell Holmes, Jr., was ninety when he retired in 1932! Obviously, those who are to hold such an important job for the rest of their lives have to be carefully chosen.

When a Supreme Court justice retires, a new justice is nominated by the president. The president and his staff look for a nominee who has a strong background in law and who is respected by law scholars. Usually the president is also looking for someone who seems to share his views about important constitutional questions.

Once the president has chosen a justice, a majority of the Senate must approve, or confirm, his choice. First a group of senators interviews the nominee. The questioning can go on

Justice Oliver Wendell Holmes, Jr., was one of the most famous and long-tenured justices in the history of the Court.

for many days. Then the Senate votes on whether or not the nominee is acceptable. During the history of the Supreme Court, one in every five nominees has been rejected by the Senate.

There are many possible reasons for a rejection. The nominees might have done something in the past that was not completely honest. He or she might not have enough

Vigorous debate in the Senate Judiciary Committee arose from President Ronald Reagan's appointment of Robert Bork to the Court.

experience in constitutional law to satisfy the Senate. Or the nominee's opinions might be too extreme to represent the needs and ideas of the time.

Even when a nominee is confirmed, the president cannot be sure which way the justice will vote. Supreme Court justices are under no pressure to please the president with their votes, because they are appointed for life. Many justices serve for decades. During that time, their ideas can change.

Obviously, the more justices a president is able to appoint to the Supreme Court, the more influence he will have on the nation's laws. Because the Constitution does not say how many justices the Supreme Court should have, some presidents have tried to increase the number so that they can tip the balance of the Court. Mainly because of this, the number of justices on the Court has varied from six at the first session, to five at the beginning of the nineteenth century, to ten under President Lincoln. Since 1869 the number has been fixed at nine by a congressional act.

Many Supreme Court justices become famous during their years on the Court. A justice may be remembered for writing an important opinion that changed the course of American history, such as Earl Warren's opinion outlawing school segregation. Segregation, he wrote, "causes a feeling of inferiority in black children, that inflicts damage to their hearts and minds."

The Supreme Court in 1917

Justices Louis Brandeis and Oliver Wendell Holmes, Jr., are famous for their dissenting opinions supporting the rights of individuals. Although the majority of the Court did not agree with them, their written opinions influenced future justices and, in the end, helped to outlaw child labor.

Another famous justice, Thurgood Marshall, will be remembered in history as "Mr. Civil Rights." He was the first African-American justice, appointed to the Supreme Court in 1967. Before joining the Court, he worked as a lawyer defending civil rights cases. It was Thurgood Marshall who defended Linda Brown in the Supreme Court and helped to end segregation in schools.

Justice Louis Brandeis

The most important justice on the Court is the chief justice, whose job it is to run the Court, providing guidance and direction to the associate justices. One of the most famous Supreme Court chief justices, John Marshall, is remembered both for his ability as a strong leader of the

Thurgood Marshall as chief counsel for the NAACP was instrumental in fighting to end segregation in U.S. schools. Here, Marshall sits on the steps to the Supreme Court with students from Little Rock, Arkansas, in 1958.

As solicitor general, Thurgood Marshall (on right) fought six southern states that wanted the Voting Rights Act of 1965 overturned. The disputed act removed unfair barriers to voting polls for blacks that were common in the South.

Court between 1801 and 1835, and for his role in increasing the Court's power. It was Marshall who made the historic statement that it is "emphatically" the job of the judicial branch "to say what the law is." During his term as chief justice, Marshall wrote more than five thousand opinions. Born in 1755 in a log cabin in Virginia, he had no formal schooling, but was a patriot who served under George Washington in the Revolutionary War.

Many things have changed in the Court, and in the nation, since John Marshall's time. In 1981, the first woman justice, Sandra Day O'Connor, was appointed to the Supreme Court. In 1991 Clarence Thomas became the youngest justice ever to be appointed to the Court. If Justice Thomas retires at the age of eighty-five in the year 2032, he will have served for forty years. By then, you could be a grandparent in a world very different from the world of today.

Yet, although times change, the nine justices who sit in the Marble Palace still follow many of the same traditions that Marshall's court followed nearly two centuries ago. They still sign their opinions using quill pens with goose feathers. They

The first eight chief justices of the U.S. Supreme Court (opposite page): (top) John Jay, John Rutledge, Oliver Ellsworth; (center) John Marshall, Roger Brook Taney; (bottom) Salmon Portland Chase, Morrison R. Waite, Melville W. Fuller.

(opposite page) President Ronald Reagan appointed the first woman to the Supreme Court, Sandra Day O'Connor. (above) After tumultuous Senate committee hearings that rocked the nation, Clarence Thomas was sworn in as a justice in 1991.

still wear black robes and hats. And they still call each other "brethren" or "brothers." Perhaps when the Court enters the twenty-first century and begins to discuss questions that we haven't even thought of yet, the justices will still follow those same traditions that were introduced on a wintry day in 1790.

The Supreme Court in December 1993: (back row from left) Associate Justices Clarence Thomas, Anthony Kennedy, David Souter, and Ruth Bader Ginsburg; (front row from left) Associate Justices Sandra Day O'Connor and Harry Blackmun, Chief Justice William Rehnquist, and Associate Justices John Paul Stevens and Antonin Scalia.

Supreme Court Justices

Name	Term	Appointed by
Chief Justices		
John Jay	1789–1795	Washington
John Rutledge	1795	Washington
Oliver Ellsworth	1796–1800	Washington
John Marshall	1801–1835	John Adams
Roger B. Taney	1836–1864	Jackson
Salmon P. Chase	1864–1873	Lincoln
Morrison R. Waite	1874–1888	Grant
Melville W. Fuller	1888–1910	Cleveland
Edward D. White	1910–1921	Taft
William H. Taft	1921–1930	Harding
Charles E. Hughes	1930–1941	Hoover
Harlan F. Stone	1941–1946	Franklin D. Roosevelt
Frederick M. Vinson	1946–1953	Truman
Earl Warren	1953–1969	Eisenhower
Warren E. Burger	1969–1986	Nixon
William H. Rehnquist	1986–	Reagan
Associate Justices		
James Wilson	1789–1798	Washington
John Rutledge	1789–1791	Washington
William Cushing	1790–1796	Washington
John Blair	1790–1796	Washington

James Iredell	1790–1799	Washington
Thomas Johnson	1792–1793	Washington
William Paterson	1793–1806	Washington
Samuel Chase	1796–1811	Washington
Bushrod Washington	1799–1829	John Adams
Alfred Moore	1800–1804	John Adams
William Johnson	1804–1834	Jefferson
H. Brockholst Livingston	1807–1823	Jefferson
Thomas Todd	1807–1826	Jefferson
Gabriel Duvall	1811–1835	Madison
Joseph Story	1812–1845	Madison
Smith Thompson	1823–1843	Monroe
Robert Trimble	1826–1828	John Quincy Adams
John McLean	1830–1861	Jackson
Henry Baldwin	1830–1844	Jackson
James M. Wayne	1835–1867	Jackson
Philip P. Barbour	1836–1841	Jackson
John Catron	1837–1865	Van Buren
John McKinley	1838–1852	Van Buren
Peter V. Daniel	1842–1860	Van Buren
Samuel Nelson	1845–1872	Tyler
Levi Woodbury	1845–1851	Polk
Robert C. Grier	1846–1870	Polk
Benjamin R. Curtis	1851–1857	Fillmore
John A. Campbell	1853–1861	Pierce
Nathan Clifford	1858–1881	Buchanan
Noah H. Swayne	1862–1881	Lincoln
Samuel F. Miller	1862–1890	Lincoln
David Davis	1862–1877	Lincoln
Stephen J. Field	1863–1897	Lincoln
William Strong	1870–1880	Grant

Joseph P. Bradley	1870–1892	Grant
Ward Hunt	1873–1882	Grant
John M. Harlan	1877–1911	Hayes
William B. Woods	1881–1887	Hayes
Stanley Matthews	1881–1889	Garfield
Horace Gray	1882–1902	Arthur
Samuel Blatchford	1882–1893	Arthur
Lucius Q.C. Lamar	1888–1893	Cleveland
David J. Brewer	1890–1910	Harrison
Henry B. Brown	1891–1906	Harrison
George Shiras, Jr.	1892–1903	Harrison
Howell E. Jackson	1893–1895	Harrison
Edward D. White	1894–1910	Cleveland
Rufus W. Peckham	1896–1909	Cleveland
Joseph McKenna	1898–1925	McKinley
Oliver W. Holmes, Jr.	1902–1932	Theodore Roosevelt
William R. Day	1903–1922	Theodore Roosevelt
William H. Moody	1906–1910	Theodore Roosevelt
Horace H. Lurton	1910–1914	Taft
Charles E. Hughes	1910–1916	Taft
Willis Van Devanter	1911–1937	Taft
Joseph R. Lamar	1911–1916	Taft
Mahlon Pitney	1912–1922	Taft
James C. McReynolds	1914–1941	Wilson
Louis D. Brandeis	1916–1939	Wilson
John H. Clarke	1916–1922	Wilson
George Sutherland	1922–1938	Harding
Pierce Butler	1923–1939	Harding
Edward T. Sanford	1923–1930	Harding
Harlan F. Stone	1925–1941	Coolidge
Owen J. Roberts	1930–1945	Hoover

Benjamin N. Cardozo	1932–1938	Hoover
Hugo L. Black	1937–1971	Franklin D. Roosevelt
Stanley F. Reed	1938–1957	Franklin D. Roosevelt
Felix Frankfurter	1939–1962	Franklin D. Roosevelt
William O. Douglas	1939–1975	Franklin D. Roosevelt
Frank Murphy	1940–1949	Franlin D. Roosevelt
James F. Byrnes	1941–1942	Franklin D. Roosevelt
Robert H. Jackson	1941–1954	Franklin D. Roosevelt
Wiley B. Rutledge	1943–1949	Franklin D. Roosevelt
Harold H. Burton	1945–1958	Truman
Tom C. Clark	1949–1967	Truman
Sherman Minton	1949–1956	Truman
John M. Harlan	1955–1971	Eisenhower
William J. Brennan, Jr.	1956–1990	Eisenhower
Charles E. Whittaker	1957–1962	Eisenhower
Potter Stewart	1958–1981	Eisenhower
Byron R. White	1962–1993	Kennedy
Arthur J. Goldberg	1962–1965	Kennedy
Abe Fortas	1965–1969	Johnson
Thurgood Marshall	1967–1991	Johnson
Harry A. Blackmun	1970–1994	Nixon
Lewis F. Powell, Jr.	1972–1987	Nixon
William H. Rehnquist	1972–1986	Nixon
John P. Stevens	1975–	Ford
Sandra Day O'Connor	1981–	Reagan
Antonin Scalia	1986–	Reagan
Anthony M. Kennedy	1988–	Reagan
David H. Souter	1990–	Bush
Clarence Thomas	1991–	Bush
Ruth Bader Ginsburg	1993–	Clinton
Stephen Breyer	1994–	Clinton

For Further Reading

Bernstein, Richard, and Jerome Agel. *Supreme Court.*
New York: Walker & Company, 1989.

Friedman, Leon. *The Supreme Court.* New York: Chelsea
House, 1987.

Green, Carl, and William Sanford. *Judiciary.* Vero Beach, Fla.:
Rourke Corporation, 1990.

Patrick, John J. *The Young Oxford Companion to the Supreme
Court of the United States.* New York: Oxford University Press,
1993.

Weiss, Ann E. *The Supreme Court.* New York: Enslow
Publishers, 1987.

Index

About the Author

Barbara Aria is a freelance writer living in New York City. She has written several books for parents and a series of articles for children studying the English language. She has also written on cultural and design-related subjects. She is married to a photographer and has a twelve-year-old daughter.